# ANNA'S
# SPECIAL PRESENT

Yoriko Tsutsui
*pictures by* Akiko Hayashi

PUFFIN BOOKS

One day Anna came home from
school with her best friend, Susie.
They were going to play with
Anna's very special doll, Emily.
But when Anna went to look for
her she had disappeared.
"I bet Katy's got her. She's always
taking my Emily away.
Katy! I want Emily back!
Give her back to me!"

Then Anna's mother came out of
the bedroom carrying Katy.
"Shush, Anna! Katy's asleep – she's
not feeling well."
"What's the matter with her?"
"I don't know," her mother said,
"but I am taking her across the
street to the doctor now. Here's
Emily back. Please be good girls
and play here quietly by yourselves
until I get back. I won't be long."

Anna and Susie played at being
doctors looking after Emily. Soon
Anna's mother came back alone.
She looked very worried.
"Katy had to go to the hospital.
The doctors think they will have to
take out her appendix."
"Will they have to cut her tummy?"
"Yes, Anna, but they will sew it up
as good as new. They are very good
doctors, so there's no need to worry."

Anna's mother went into their bedroom and packed a bag for Katy.

"I've got to take Katy her night clothes."

"When will she be back?" Anna asked.

"She may be in the hospital for several days, but you can go and see her. Don't worry, Anna. She'll be well soon. Now, listen. Mrs Thomas across the corridor will keep an eye on you until Daddy gets back. I've just talked to him on the phone and he'll be home very soon. Will you and Susie be all right until he gets back? I have to go to the hospital."

"Mmm..."

Anna and Susie played with Emily some more. Suddenly the sky grew dark, and the wind blew through the windows. Daddy hadn't come home yet.

"I should go home before it starts to rain," said Susie.

"Please stay a little longer. Daddy will be home soon."

But the sky grew darker and darker.

"I've got to go now. It's going to rain."

Anna was left all alone.

The wind grew stronger and it
began to rain. Suddenly there was
a flash of lightning and a huge
crack of thunder. Anna was
frightened. Daddy still hadn't come
home. She ran and hid under her
blanket, clutching Emily.
"Don't be frightened, Emily. I'm
here to look after you. We're not
scared of thunder, are we? And
Katy will be better soon."
It was so warm that soon she fell
asleep.

Suddenly the lights went on and
Anna woke up. Daddy walked into
the room and sat down next to
Anna.
"Anna, dear, I'm sorry I'm late. You
must have been frightened."
He gave her a big hug.
"Let's go and have something to eat."

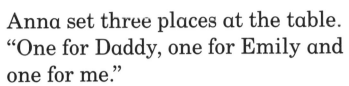

Anna set three places at the table.
"One for Daddy, one for Emily and
one for me."
Then the phone rang. Daddy picked
it up.
"Hello! How is she? Oh . . . thank
goodness! Anna!"
Anna went to the phone. Her
mother sounded funny and a very
long way off.
"Hello, Anna. Katy's had her
operation. She's still sleeping, but
she'll wake up soon. I'm going to
stay with her tonight, and you and
Daddy can come and see her
tomorrow. Is that all right?"
"Okay," Anna said in a very small
voice.

Anna's father slept in Katy's bed
that night.
Anna woke up very early the next
morning.
"I wonder what I can take to the
hospital for Katy."
She found a box of bright paper and
began folding it into pretty shapes
like flowers and birds. But then she
had an even better idea.
"I know what I can give Katy!
Something she'd really like!"
Anna began to wrap up a big
parcel.

That afternoon Anna and her
father went to the hospital.

They were shown into Katy's room.
There she was in bed with a tube
attached to her arm. She looked
very happy to see them.
"Daddy! Anna!"

The nurse came and took the tube
from Katy's arm.
"What's that you've got, Anna?"
asked her mother.
Anna went over to Katy. She
handed her the package.
"Here, Katy, this is for you."

"Oh, look! A letter and some paper flowers and birds. But what's this?" Katy tore the pretty wrapping paper from Anna's present.

"Emily! Oh, Anna, are you really
giving me Emily?"
Anna held her breath.
She nodded yes.

"Thank you, thank you!" said Katy.
Anna's mother squeezed her tight
and said, "Anna, you are so kind.
What a lovely present. How
grown-up you are!"
And Katy tucked Emily up in bed
right beside her.

PUFFIN BOOKS
A division of Penguin Books USA Inc.
375 Hudson Street, New York, New York 10014
Penguin Books Ltd, 27 Wrights Lane, London W8 5TZ, England
Penguin Books Australia Ltd, Ringwood, Victoria, Australia
Penguin Books Canada Ltd, 2801 John Street, Markham, Ontario, Canada L3R 1B4
Penguin Books (N.Z.) Ltd, 182–190 Wairau Road, Auckland 10, New Zealand

Penguin Books Ltd, Registered Offices: Harmondsworth, Middlesex, England

First published in Japan by Fukuinkan Shoten Publishers Inc., Tokyo, 1983
First published in the United States of America by Viking Penguin,
a division of Penguin Books USA Inc., 1988
Published in Picture Puffins, 1990
1  3  5  7  9  10  8  6  4  2
Text copyright © Yoriko Tsutsui, 1983   Illustrations copyright © Akiko Hayashi, 1983
All rights reserved

LIBRARY OF CONGRESS CATALOGING IN PUBLICATION DATA
Tsutsui, Yoriko.   Anna's special present.
Summary: Anna hates it when her little sister Katy
begs to play with her favorite doll; but, when Katy is
sick in the hospital, Anna knows just the right gift to cheer her.
[1. Sisters—Fiction.  2. Dolls—Fiction.  3. Sick—
Fiction]  I. Hayashi, Akiko, 1945–   ill.  II. Title.
PZ7.T795An  1990    [E]    89-10844
ISBN 0-14-054219-1
Printed in Hong Kong